Red Ranger Came Calling

BERKELEY BREATHED

Red Ranger Came Calling

A Guaranteed True Christmas Story

Little, Brown and Company

Boston New York Toronto London

Deepest thanks and a solemn salute to Ray Singer, who recognized his duty as
a proper space ranger and let us plunder his wonderful collection of
memorabilia for the jacket and cover photographs.

Copyright © 1994 by Berkeley Breathed

First Edition

Back cover photograph, *Red Breathed and Son;*
and bike-in-tree photograph, page 46: Jody Boyman
Cover memorabilia photographs: Dixie Knight

ISBN 0-316-10881-2
Library of Congress Catalog Card Number 94-76137

10 9 8 7 6 5 4 3 2

LAKE

Published simultaneously in Canada by Little, Brown & Company (Canada)
Limited
Printed in the United States of America

Write to Berkeley Breathed
in care of Little, Brown and Company,
34 Beacon St., Boston, MA 02108

To my father, the Red Ranger, of course.

He's finally up there somewhere, just off Pluto maybe.

IN 1939, MY FATHER WAS NINE YEARS OLD. THEN, AND FOR THE REST OF HIS LIFE, HE WAS CALLED RED BY EVERYONE BUT HIS MOTHER, WHO THOUGHT THE NAME SAUCY. PEOPLE GUESSED WRONGLY THAT THE NAME HONORED THE THATCH OF ORANGE DEBRIS ATOP HIS HEAD THAT MADE IT LOOK LIKE A FRECKLED OSTRICH EGG ON FIRE. THE NAME'S TRUE SOURCE WAS A POPULAR CINEMA HERO OF THE TIME: BUCK TWEED, THE RED RANGER OF MARS, PROTECTOR OF THE 23RD CENTURY AND SAVIOR OF GRATEFUL PRINCESSES.

IT WAS HE, THE RED RANGER FROM THE MOVIES, THAT MY FATHER CHOSE TO CONFUSE WITH HIMSELF. AND IT WAS THAT UNIVERSE, CLUTTERED WITH SPACE NAZIS AND PRINCESS NABBERS, THAT SEEMED TO NEED HIM MORE THAN HIS OWN. BUT THE KEY TO SUCH A WORLD STILL ELUDED HIM: AN OFFICIAL BUCK TWEED TWO-SPEED CRIME-STOPPER STAR-HOPPER BICYCLE.

IT IS WITH A BICYCLE THAT THIS STORY BEGINS AND ENDS - A STORY THAT MY FATHER, THE FORMER RED RANGER OF MARS, TOLD US ON THE CHRISTMAS EVES OF MY OWN CHILDHOOD. I'VE PUT HIS ADVENTURE TO PICTURES HERE, ITS HISTORICAL TRUTH GUARAN- TEED BY THE RED RANGER HIMSELF. BUT TRUTH, LIKE THE DAYDREAMS OF NINE-YEAR-OLD BOYS, IS SLIPPERY AND PRONE TO READJUSTMENT OVER TIME.

I CAN ONLY SUBMIT TO YOU THE TALE ITSELF AS HE TOLD IT IN HIS OWN WORDS . . . PLUS THE EVIDENCE STILL THERE IN THE FOREST, OF COURSE.

Berkeley Breathed

APRIL 1994

Christmas, 1939

During the Depression years, before the second war, my folks would banish me from East Orange, New Jersey, to Michigan for the school year and then ship me to upstate New York for summer camp. The lone remaining month, for Christmas, would find me on a train to my aunt Vy's house, on Vashon, a damp little island somewhere off the country's upper left-hand corner. It was an out-of-the-way corner, but a good place to grow things, where strawberries and sour-faced little boys might ripen up sweeter. Or so my mother told me each time she sent me away.

But on Christmas Eve of 1939, I'd grown no sweeter at all. My prize eluded me: an Official Buck Tweed Two-Speed Crime-Stopper Star-Hopper bicycle. It sat there gleaming in the Vashon Hardware Store window, tantalizing earthlings with its spine-tingling glamour.

The Red Ranger of Mars — me — visited this place daily, like a cow returning to a salt lick. There I would loiter, miserable in bicycle poverty, kept company by Amelia, Aunt Vy's dalmation wiener-dog mix. Most of the time Amelia just snoozed nearby, dreaming, like me, of other places and other lives far away.

But it was 1939, and although Christmas Eve had arrived, dreams were unaffordable. Amelia and I headed home with mine far behind in a store window.

As usual, I looked for delays on the walk home. Aunt Vy would be waiting, and we made each other equally uncomfortable, so I saw no reason to hurry. That evening's detour brought me and Amelia past the ramshackle lighthouse perched high in the mist on Point Robinson. As always, we paused to consider the old house's legend.

Island old-timers insisted that its unseen occupant, old Saunder Clös, was actually *Santa Claus himself* . . . the real McCoy of childish fancy migrated down from the North to spend his final days in secretive retirement on Vashon Island.

It took folks far more fruity than the Red Ranger of Mars to be tricked into believing such twaddle. Like many my age, I knew that Santa Claus and the tooth fairy and the Easter bunny were just that many more promises hatched by those who weren't very good at keeping any.

As we turned to leave, an astonishingly squat little man no bigger than me rushed past us toward the old lighthouse. He carried an overnight carpetbag, which bumped along behind him. The tiny man smiled weakly and tipped his hat, revealing *pointy* ears. Something flowery needed to be said by the Red Ranger of Mars, but in my shock, all that came out was "Mister, you look like a turnip."

I could not recall ever actually seeing a genuine elf, nor calling one a vegetable, but I was certain that I just had. An elf. You-know-who's elf. To a dyed-in-the-wool everything doubter such as myself, it was mind-boggling.

That evening Aunt Vy asked me to help pin up some old holiday magazine pictures, but I declined, as my mind had been freshly boggled. Vy noticed my peculiar mood and offered to let me open my Christmas gift from her early. It was a glorious Buck Tweed space uniform, the bonus highlight being a large red *R* zooming across the breastplate. I tried it on, and she flung a hand across her brow, swooning from the swashbuckling drama of it all. We had finally discovered our first bit of common ground.

But my space ranger senses detected that the jersey was in truth last year's cast-off pajama top, dyed Ranger red and altered by the loving hands of its giver. "Pajamas," I said with crushing disappointment. I didn't speak again, but my fingers explored the familiar cloth and my expression hid none of my defeat. Vy turned away, hiding her own.

I did not typically give much thought to the feelings of others, and — true to form — I did not that night. My mother used to tell me that there was a natural order to all things and that mine must have been prickliness. She said that blaming me — or anybody else — for my distant nature would be like blaming a polar bear for eating Canadians. It was the natural order and that was that.

I thought of this as I went up to bed.

As I lay there in the dark, my thoughts
returned to the earlier elf sighting. He had looked
like the real thing. And elves to Santa Claus are
like horseflies to a horse: one means that the other
is nearby. For a child, even me, it was all too
tempting to believe. But then, wasn't everything?
And everybody? It occurred to me that a kid's life
was one long opportunity for having the rug pulled
out from below him at every step. Myself, I was
determined to stay on my feet.

Still, a fraud was surely afoot, and it was the
sworn duty of the Red Ranger of Mars to stick his
nose deep into such things.

Amelia followed, looking doubtful, as I dropped
out my window. I bent low and then crept off into
the island fog to unmask a humbug.

The Saunder Clös house teetered high above the
pounding surf, the moon igniting the rising mist
into blue phosphorescence. Ancient toys in
disrepair littered the steps like ghosts from a baby's
bad dream. We clambered past an old sign nailed
into the rock:

Visitors
Not Received
With Zesty
Jolliness
at the moment.

I almost turned back right there. I was growing
uneasy about the whole matter, and a public
guarantee of grumpiness didn't help. I knocked on
the huge door, unzestfully.

The big door swung open slowly on rusty hinges. The little pointy-eared old man from before stood there holding a tea tray, scowling. The light from an enormous fire behind him made the room flicker with grotesque shadows. My thoughts turned to retreat, but instead, I stood at attention. "The Red Ranger has come calling," I said, and bowed deeply over shaking knees.

The little man scowled further but motioned for us to enter. The terrible shadows were caused by monstrous toys looming in dark corners. And dozing in a fantastic chair was what I figured to be old Saunder Clös, the most ancient man I had ever seen. He coughed quietly and breathed with a rattling wheeze of great antiquity. His body, shrunken and folded, looked as though it had retreated from life itself. Before I could announce myself again, he spoke without looking up. "Turn around," he said in a voice the age of the mountains. "Go home. Go back to bed. What you're looking for isn't here. I'm 435 years old, which makes me . . . very tired."

Even in my mounting terror, I was grateful to meet another skilled liar. "I'm Buck Tweed, the Red Ranger of Mars, 602 years old," I said, adding as a bonus, "and I do not believe at all in Santa Claus."

With that, the little elf shuddered and looked in horror to his master, whose eyes had ignited. The old man began to push himself up from his huge chair, and he finally looked at me, glowering. Frankly, this was more than I could take. I panicked and shot the old faker with my disintegrator ray gun.

The old man sank back into his chair, stunned, as if a tuna fish were stuck to his forehead and not a dart. He pulled it off, then motioned with a bony hand for me to approach. I did, deeply regretting my violence. When I got close, he took my pistol and held it up gingerly for a better look. His eyes widened. "Never," he said, "have I made such a thing. What is it for?"

His question brought me back to comfortable territory, masking my panic. I said, "Why, I've shot down a fleet of Nazi attack ships with that. I've mowed down a mob of Venusian Hottentots. I've even burned a hole through Mars's moon and singed fannies on Pluto." I had been infected with the room's atmosphere of malarky. I gave him another chance to hatch one himself. "They say you're Santa Claus," I said.

His face darkened. "Santa Claus," he said, repeating the name as though it hurt. His eyes looked ahead and seemed to focus beyond the walls. "He's a foolish story for small children. He's a big jolly bribe to control their natural criminal instincts." He chuckled at this without smiling. "It's been that way for a long time. But it wasn't always . . ." His eyes focused back on me. Smiling sadly, he said, "He's old now. And the times are newer . . . *people* are newer." He studied my ray gun again. "Who'd believe now?"

"I'd believe," I said, but I wasn't sure at all. I had to see what the old fruitcake had up his sleeve. "I'd believe . . . if he could make a reindeer fly."

For the first time, a light brightened in his eyes. The elf looked appalled and whispered, "Don't do it, boss. You're not 300 anymore." The old man wasn't listening as he pushed himself out of the chair and settled his weight on wobbly knees. He shuffled over to the fireplace mantel and held his hands around a little carved reindeer. Scrunching his eyes, he made a great effort to do something, although I couldn't tell what. After several minutes of nothing happening, the old man rested on his elbows, exhausted. "Blast," he said in frustration, just as the elf dropped his tea tray. We turned around, and I heard the old man say, "Oops." Amelia was drifting slowly up toward the ceiling like a leaky balloon. If a dog can look unamused, she did. And if a space ranger can look dumb-founded and thrilled at the same time, then I did, too.

Even a hard nut such as myself sometimes had to consider overwhelming evidence, odd as it was. My mind was saying that I was fixing to get another rug pulled out from below me, but my eyes were saying that a dog was floating in the rafters. The tug-of-war inside made me light-headed, and through a fog of confusion, I heard myself say, "I have a wish."

The old man's eyes lit up fully this time. The elf looked freshly appalled. "Don't do it, boss. It's been a long time. Let's just get you to bed." The old man waved him off and turned to look at me as if he was starving and I was holding a boysenberry pie.

Like an old actor reciting lines from his youth, he said, "So, what would you like for Christmas?"

I was already at the edge, so I leapt: "An Official Buck Tweed Two-Speed Crime-Stopper Star-Hopper bicycle," I said. He frowned and looked at me as if I'd asked for a blue cantaloupe. I described my prize again, saying each word slowly and louder. He bent down over the back of the elf and cupped his ear. I made it simple: "I'd like a Tweed bicycle."

"That's what you want? You're quite sure?" he said, looking surprised.

"I'm sure. A Tweed bicycle. It's the latest thing."

The old man straightened up and scratched his head. "I'll try my best," he said, grinning.

I roped Amelia and hauled her down from the overhead beams. She was near emotional collapse during the walk home but then I was too.

On Christmas morning I awoke to the air colored pink, which I took as a sign of coming paradise. Slipping down the hall, I paused and crossed my fingers for luck before viewing the prize that would guarantee my happiness into old age.

Amelia lay spread-eagled and snoring on the rug, safely anchored to earth by a toaster and a Hoover vacuum cleaner. Our pitiful tree was tucked against the wall, looking lonely and pitiful as usual. Also as usual, the room was empty of Buck Tweed bicycles. Completely, utterly, terribly empty.

I searched the house and yard, confirming the worst. No bicycle. With a few flashy parlor tricks, the old humbug had steered me right into the same old childish quicksand: faith in a grown-up. My disappointment bubbled into anger, and I vowed out loud that Mr. Santa Phony Claus would feel the terrible wrath of the Red Ranger of Mars.

Amelia wanted no part of wraths and tried crawling farther under the Hoover, but I scooped her up and stomped off in a rage toward the old house on Point Robinson.

As we made our way over the fresh snow, out of my mouth poured a symphony of childhood outrage so fiery in passion, so shocking in fury that it super-heated the morning air. Behind me it left a great purple fog of cussing residue wafting across the Vashon strawberry fields. Some say it's still drifting about today, causing panic among the rabbits.

We reached the house, and I stormed in without knocking. I barely noticed that sheets covered the paintings and windows in the hall. I found the old phony upstairs in bed.

But there were others in the room. More elves. A swarm of elves. A flock, a flood, a murmuring horde of puny pointy-eared little old men stood about with their hats off. Although foggy-minded in my fury, I couldn't help but be impressed with such a scene.

I affixed a double deadly Red Ranger evil eye on the old man in bed. He breathed with a whistling rattle and opened his eyes when I stopped at the door. "Boys," he wheezed, "the Red Ranger has come calling." Looking at me, he said, "We're having a going-away party, Red. These old friends were kind enough to see me off."

His arms rose shakily, outstretched. His eyebrows went high, as if waiting for some sort of wonderful news. "Come closer," he said, eyes glistening. "Tell me *exactly* what you thought of your special bicycle."

Ohhhhh. I'd tell him *exactly* all right.

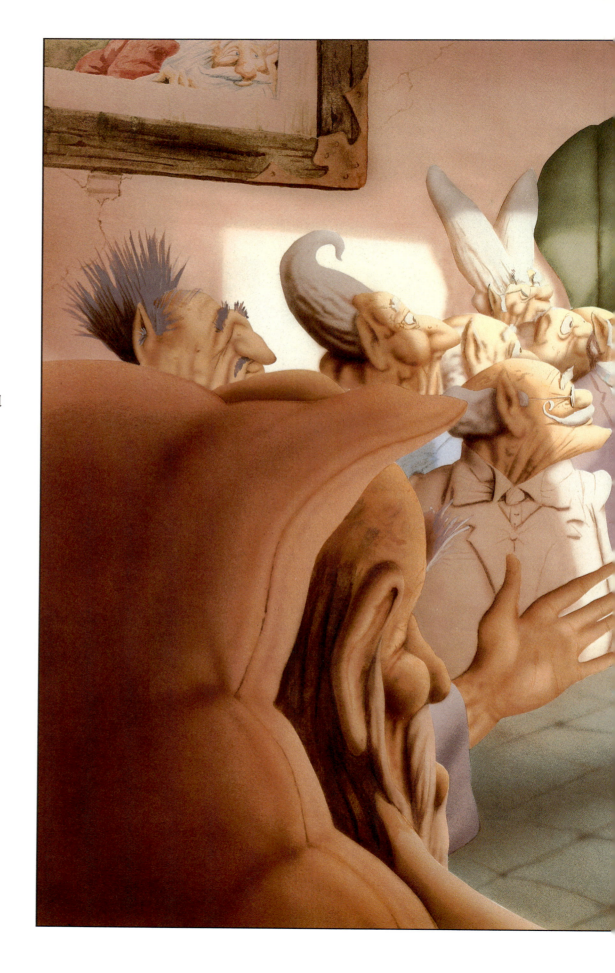

I paused to organize my fit. But as the steam built up and the vile words arranged themselves, a new emotion began to build, pushing aside my anger. I fought it back, but to my horror, it kept coming. The Red Ranger of Mars, protector of the 23rd century and savior of grateful princesses, faced a new enemy: tears. As I think back now, after so many years, it seems they came for more than just a bicycle beyond reach.

But before they arrived, the old man's hand reached out toward my own. Years of brainless kid instinct obscured my emotions, and I grasped it.

Even through my brimming tantrum, I noticed it was damp and trembling. His eyes stared at mine, looking for a word of Red Ranger approval. They seemed to beg for it. Why, ol' Saunder Clös was *nervous.* The sad, failing old man — whoever he was — truly believed he'd delivered to me my Christmas wish.

And then up from some unexplored crevice inside me, from a place that I did not know, came something new in my experience. I opened my mouth and watched helpless as it all poured out.

"The bicycle! Of course, *that* bicycle! Sir, I have never quite had such a glorious machine in all my life! You may have noticed my face actually glowing just now! That was from pride!" Using skills gained over a lifetime of telling whoppers, I launched into a soaring account of the adventures I planned aboard a bicycle that I knew I did not have. His eyes blazed to life with each growing fiction, meeting each swoop from the truth with clapping hands and a triumphant "Woooee!"

After I finished, I sat back, winded from the torrent of joyful fibbery. I was feeling strangely happy while it occurred to me that I had no particular reason to be happy at all. "Let's go home," I said to Amelia, who jumped. She hadn't seen me smile before and figured I was having a seizure.

As we turned to leave, I noticed that the elves seemed agitated. At the door, I looked back to see several of them trying gently to keep the old man in his bed. Color had temporarily filled his cheeks, and he struggled to his feet. Grinning impishly, he motioned for silence and then bent to elf-ear level. He whispered, "Boys, we're back." The little men looked mortified.

Turning to me, he smiled and said, "It's been a pleasure having the Red Ranger call."

I saluted and said, "Then I'll call again." I meant it, but that's the last I ever saw of the old man.

As I headed for the stairs, he had summoned up the last of his strength and stood at the door, his arms outstretched. "Time to fly!" he said. Slowly, every one of the gathered elves gently drifted out of his room and up toward the rafters, the expression on their faces looking similar to the one I'd seen on Amelia's the night before. I pried my copilot out of the corner, where she was wedged in mortal horror, and we left, my head reeling.

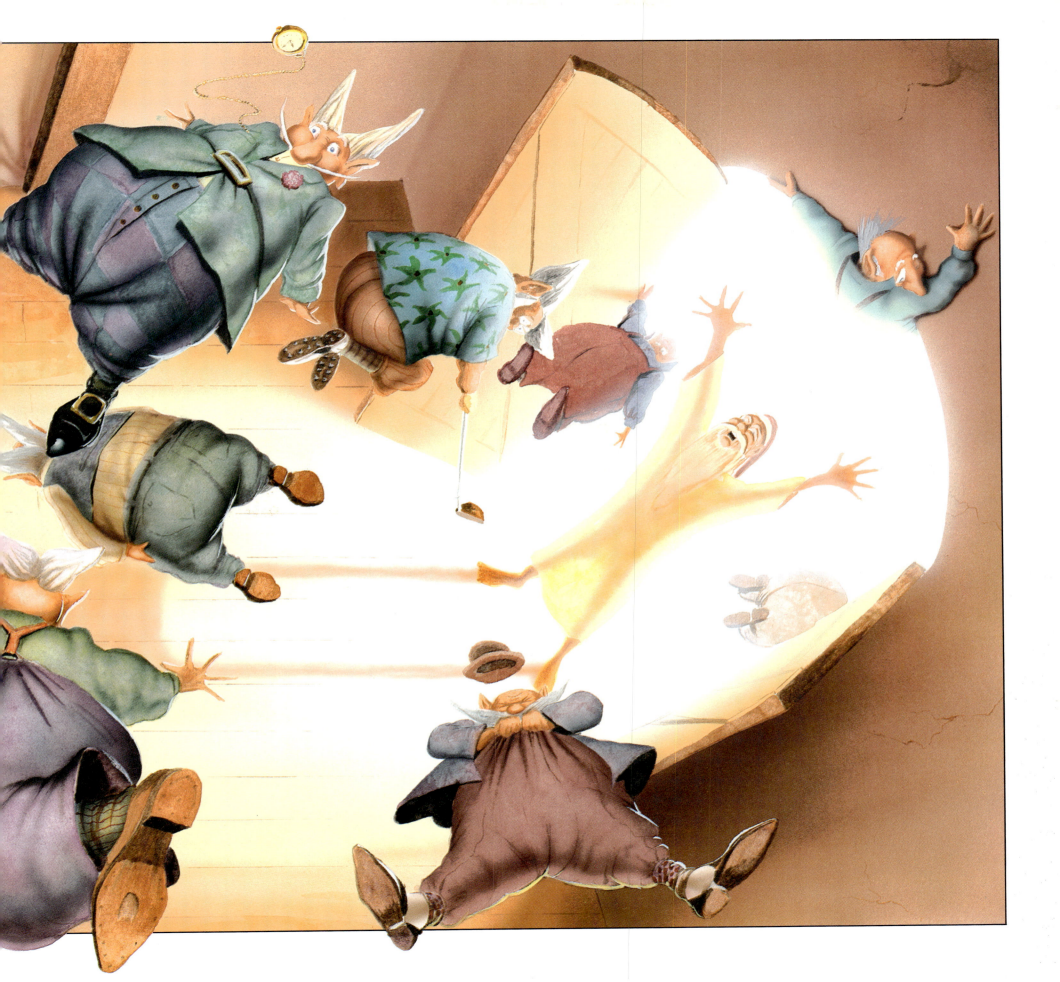

I discovered it on the way home that morning. It had been in my front yard all the time — I just hadn't thought to look *up*. Neighbors had also begun to notice and silently approached. If a dog can look flabbergasted, Amelia did.

The morning breeze spun the front wheel lazily while I stared up in open-mouthed astonishment.

A shiny brand-new bicycle, custom-made just for me, glimmered in the morning sun . . . piercing the trunk of Vashon Island's oldest fir tree. It sat there, ten feet up, pointing precisely toward the North Pole, as it would for the rest of all time.

So if not exactly a *Tweed* bicycle, then surely a *treed* one . . . placed there by a strange old man whose ears failed him before his heart did.

In the days and years ahead, I would think often of how that useless bicycle had been an answer to both our wishes, my own being one I'd never admitted. But on that Christmas morning of 1939, I knew only that I needed to wake Aunt Vy up and tell her how extraordinarily fond I was of an old cast-off pajama top dyed Ranger red.

Fifty years later, if you ask if I'm not making this all up, I'll say this: The word of the Red Ranger of Mars should be all you need. And if you ask if I believe in Santa Claus, I'll say this: Mind your own business. And if you ask about that tree on a Christmas morning a lifetime ago, the one holding the last little bit of an old man's faith and the first of a sour-faced little boy's, I'll say this . . .

It's still there.